WE CAN SAVE THE EARTH

THE LAND WE LIVE ON

Written by:
Jill Wheeler

COMMUNITY BAPTIST CHRISTIAN SCHOOL
5715 MIAMI ROAD
SOUTH BEND, INDIANA 46614
Phone : 219 291-3620

Published by Abdo & Daughters, 6535 Cecilia Circle, Edina, Minnesota 55439

Library bound edition distributed by Rockbottom Books, Pentagon Tower, P.O. Box 36036, Minneapolis, Minnesota 55435

Copyright© 1990 by Abdo Consulting Group, Inc., Pentagon Tower, P.O. Box 36036, Minneapolis, Minnesota 55435. International copyrights reserved in all countries. No part of this book may be reproduced in any form without written permission from the publisher. Printed in the United States.

Library of Congress Number: 90-083602   ISBN: 1-56239-003-1

Cover Illustrations by: C.A. Nobens
Interiors by: Kristi Schaeppi

Edited by: Stuart Kallen

TABLE OF CONTENTS

Introduction 5

Chapter 1 7
 Deforestation

Chapter 2 15
 Wetlands

Chapter 3 18
 Erosion

Chapter 4 22
 What You Can Do

A Final Word 29

Glossary 30

Index 31

INTRODUCTION

In the 1930's, many areas of the United States suffered from a great drought. There was so little rain and so much hot, sunny weather that the land dried up. Fields that once had been lush and green with healthy crops became dusty and barren. It appeared that the nation's farmlands were turning into huge deserts.

Eventually, the rains returned and the fields came back to life. In the meantime, people had learned the importance of the land we live on. Without good land, we cannot grow crops to feed ourselves. Without good land, animals, plants and birds will die. Healthy land is essential to the existence of everything on earth.

People have not taken good care of the land we live on. We can see the scars of human carelessness all around us.

We see that carelessness in vast acres of bare land that once supported lush tropical rainforests. We see it in the ugly, open pits caused by strip mining for coal and metals. We see it in the millions of acres of wetlands that have been drained until they no longer can provide a habitat for wild birds and animals. And we see it in land farmed carelessly until its rich topsoil has disappeared through erosion.

There still is time to repair some of the damage we have done. But we must act now. This book will help you get started on protecting and preserving the land we live on.

CHAPTER 1
Deforestation

Deforestation means to cut down and burn forests until the land is left bare. Humans have practiced deforestation for thousands of years. Most areas of modern farmland once were thick, green forests. The forests were cut down so the land could be farmed to produce food and feed animals.

There are many types of forests. They are classified according to the kind of plant and animal life that exists there. One particular kind of forest is in grave danger now because of humans — the *tropical rainforest*.

Tropical rainforests are fascinating places located near the equator in Central and South America, Africa, Asia and Australia. Rainforests get their name because so much rain falls there, sometimes more than 200 inches per year. Compare that to Chicago, which receives only about 33 inches of rain a year.

This unique weather pattern creates a special environment filled with as many as five million different species of plants and animals. This is as many as half of **all** species of plants and animals on earth.

In the last 50 years, humans have been destroying tropical rainforests at an alarming rate. Currently, rainforests are being destroyed at the rate of between 50 to 100 acres a **minute**!

People are using bulldozers and fire to level the rainforests so they can make money by grazing cattle and raising crop on the land. Already 25 million acres of rainforest has been cleared to feed cows for beef production. Tropical trees also are cut down to be made into furniture and lumber.

If this deforestation rate continues, there will be no more rainforests by the year 2050. There are many reasons why we cannot allow this to happen.

Many helpful medicines are made from plants in the rainforests. Thanks to a rainforest plant, the rosy periwinkle, the survival rates of children with leukemia have risen from 20 percent to 80 percent. In fact, nearly three-quarters of the 3,000 plants known to help fight cancer come from the tropical rainforest.

When we destroy rainforests, we also destroy species of plants and animals. Many more people would have died if the rosy periwinkle had been destroyed before its healing properties could be discovered. No one knows how many other rainforest plants hold the secret to curing other diseases. If the rainforests continue to be destroyed, no one will ever know and more people will die needlessly.

Did You Know . . .

We lose a patch of rainforest the size of New York's Central Park every sixteen minutes.

Sick people are not the only ones who benefit from rainforests. Rainforests with their giant trees and thick vegetation act as natural air filters. They absorb carbon dioxide from the air as they grow. Too much carbon dioxide traps the sun's heat in the atmosphere, raising global temperatures. This is called the *greenhouse effect*. When rainforests are destroyed, the carbon contained in the plants is released back into the air. This makes the greenhouse effect even worse.

Rainforests also help regulate the earth's water supply. They soak up heavy tropical rains and then slowly and steadily release the water from the soil. This way, there is a constant supply of water for people and animals who live around the rainforest. Rainforests even affect the weather patterns thousands of miles away.

When rainforests are destroyed, the entire climate around the rainforests changes. In addition, bulldozing and burning rainforests pollutes the nearby rivers and oceans, contaminating drinking water supplies and killing marine life.

Once rainforests are gone, the land can only be used for farming for two or three years. After that, the land is dead and useless to humans, plants or animals. In Panama, the Sariqua Desert grows 100 yards a year through land that once supported a rainforest. The land has been so harmed by overgrazing of cattle that not even grass will grow on it anymore.

Cleared rainforests also erode, create landslides and worsen flooding. This is because there is no vegetation to help the water soak into the soil, or prevent the soil from blowing or washing away. This happened in Indonesia in 1977 and 1979 when two deforested river valleys flooded. The flooding destroyed the rice fields of 10,000 farmers.

It also is important to remember the rainforests are home to more than 140 million people. These people depend on the rainforests for food and fuel. Destroying the rainforests also destroys these peoples' homes and their entire way of life.

Deforestation is not limited to tropical rainforests. Many other kinds of forests also are being destroyed, including forests in the United States. The stands of giant redwoods along America's west coast now are only 4 percent of their original size.

While most companies that cut down forests plant new trees in their place, it takes many years for these forests to grow back. Even then, the forests are never the same as the originals. The habitat for hundreds of birds, animals, and insects has been destroyed and will not return for many, many years, if ever. At the same time, cutting down the forests pollutes local water supplies and leaves no forest to filter and cleanse the rain that falls.

Just as forests help clean our environment, so does another kind of place in the land we live on. It too is in danger, as you will see in the next chapter.

CHAPTER 2
Wetlands

Most people don't pay much attention to wetlands. People often call them swamps or marshes, and some people say they are a nuisance. In reality, wetlands are very important to the land we live on.

Wetlands are natural water purifiers. They filter out chemicals and sediment, leaving water that is safe to drink. These unique areas also serve as the breeding grounds for many wild birds and fish.

Wetlands also help prevent floods. Many wetlands are located near coastal areas. They can absorb and hold excess water released by storms until the ground farther inland can handle the water without flooding.

Unfortunately, thousands of acres of wetlands are being destroyed. In the United States alone, we lose about 300,000 acres of wetlands a year. The wetlands are drained so roads, fields, mines and homes can be built. Other wetlands are destroyed when humans dump chemicals or trash into the wetlands.

As the wetlands vanish, so does their ability to cleanse water, prevent floods and serve as a home for plants, birds and fish. But the final losers in this case are humans themselves.

In the next chapter, we will read about another way humans are clouding their future by harming the land we live on.

CHAPTER 3
Erosion

If you've ever seen a large hole dug in the ground, you've noticed that soil changes color the deeper under the surface you go. The soil on the very top of the ground is called *topsoil*.

This type of soil has the most nutrients for plants because it contains organic matter. Organic matter includes parts of dead plants that provide fertilizer for new plants. It takes about 500 years for nature to produce one inch of topsoil.

Topsoil is very important to living things. If wind or water carries the topsoil away, or *erodes*, it is more difficult for plants to grow. If plants don't grow, humans and animals have little to eat.

Did You Know . . .

It takes nature about 500 years to form one inch of topsoil. Humans are losing topsoil at the rate of one inch every 19 years.

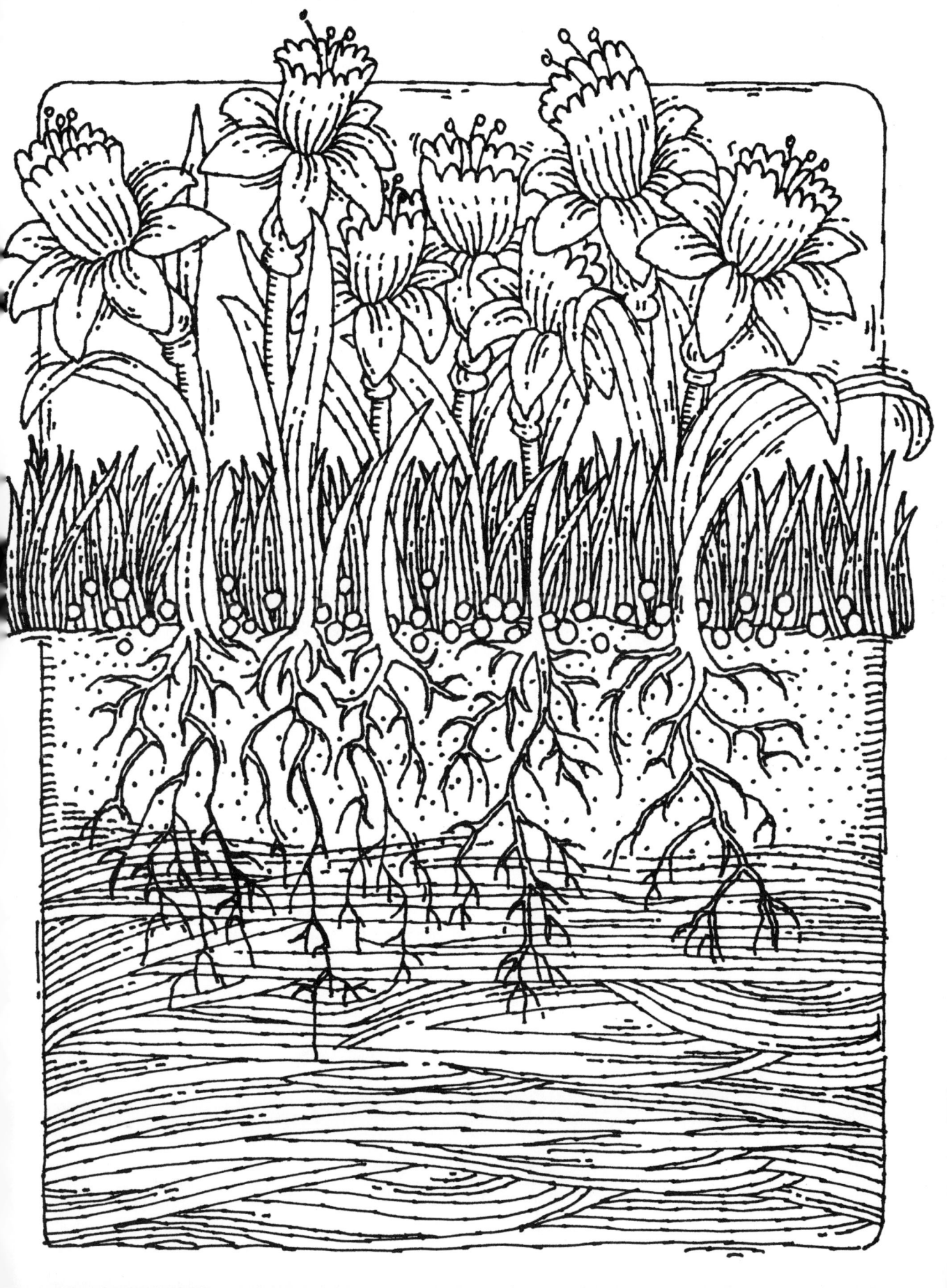

Usually, nature sees to it that topsoil does not erode. Forests, grasses and other coverings of plants protect topsoil from eroding by holding it down. These plants also help the soil catch the rains and hold the water until it can soak into the soil.

Problems arise when humans remove that natural covering of trees and other plants. When tropical rainforests are destroyed, there no longer is any vegetation to stop the water from running off the land before it can soak in. Many times, areas that once were lush forests become deserts because the rain quickly runs off the land, carrying the rich, nutritious topsoil with it.

Humans also harm the land we live on by improper farming methods that leave the land bare after the crops have been removed. The bare land is easily eroded by wind and rain, and soon does not have enough nutrients to support crops. In the United States alone, an estimated 100 million acres of cropland already has been abandoned because of damage from erosion.

Another cause of erosion is *strip mining*. In this process, miners dig shallow pits in the earth to obtain minerals and coal. Once the area has been mined, the land is left bare of any vegetation. In this state, it is easily eroded by wind and water.

Some mining companies now clean up the areas they mine so the land is protected from further damage. However, many old mining sites remain barren.

Deforestation, careless farming and strip mining all damage the land we live on. But these can be avoided, and in some cases, damage can be repaired. In the next chapter, we'll find out what everyone can do to protect and preserve this precious resource.

CHAPTER 4
What You Can Do

- Write on both sides of the paper — the less new paper we need, the fewer trees must be cut down and the longer our forests will last.

- Avoid buying anything made from tropical hardwoods such as mahogany, rosewood, satinwood or teak. Choose locally grown hardwoods instead, such as maple, oak, walnut and ash, and encourage your family and friends to do the same.

- Support local farmer's markets and family farm operations that employ *sustainable agriculture* practices, which preserve the land for future generations.

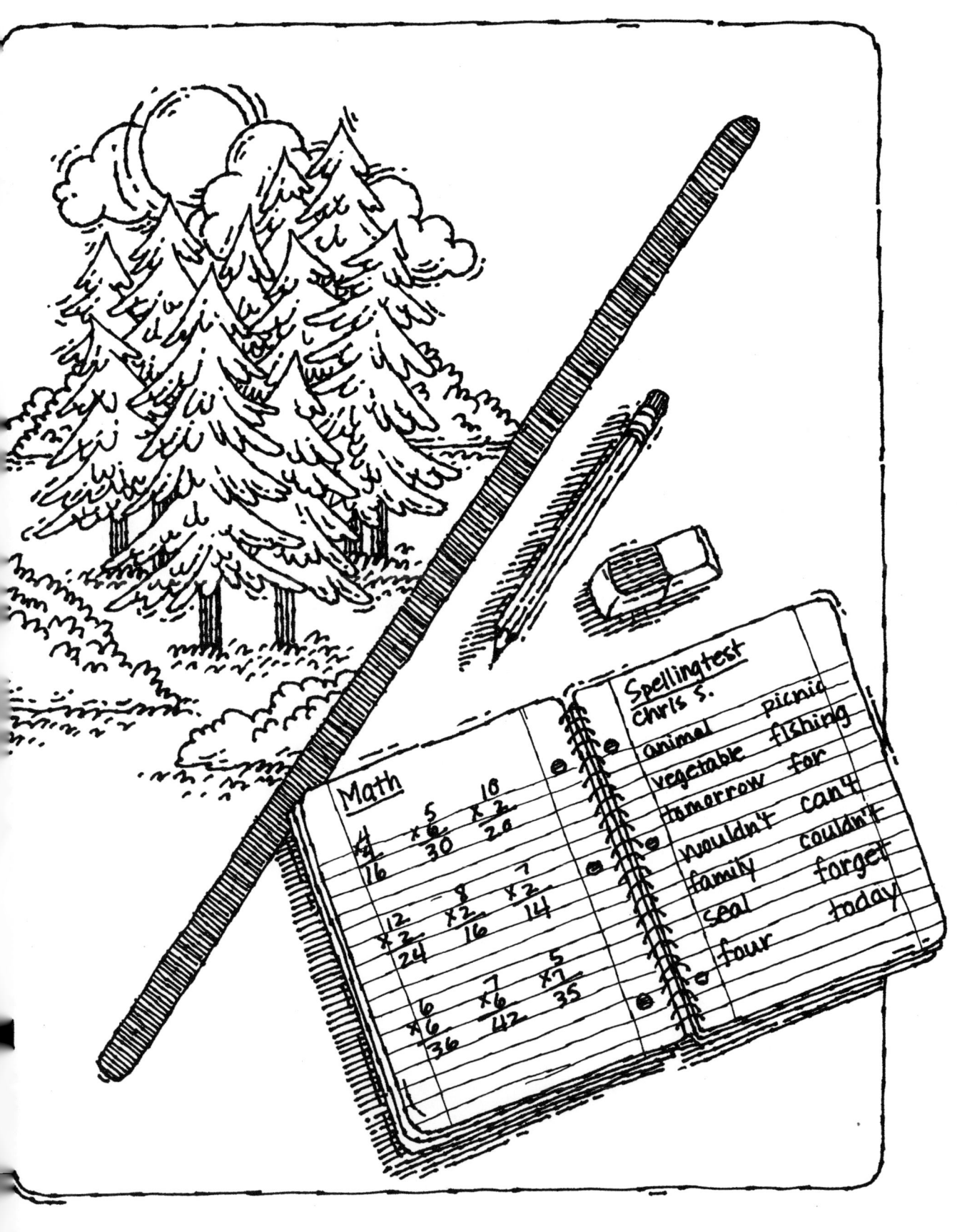

- Plant areas of bare ground with wildflowers, natural prairie grasses, bushes and trees to prevent erosion.
- Recycle!
- Avoid eating fast-food hamburgers. More than 120 million pounds of beef is imported to the U.S. from Central America each year. Most of this beef is produced on cleared rainforest land. In the U.S., the beef is used primarily in fast-food restaurants. In fact, the largest fast-food restaurant chain uses the equivalent of 16,000 cows each week.

Did You Know . . .

The amount of packaging discarded daily by each U.S. resident is 10.8 ounces.
Amount discarded by each Mexico City resident is 3.8 ounces.

- Avoid buying exotic pets such as monkeys, cockatoos, pythons and macaws. There's a good chance these animals were taken illegally from rainforests and may be endangered species.

- Get involved! Some options:

  Rainforests Action Network
  Ste. A, 301 Broadway
  San Francisco, CA 94133

  Nature Conservancy
  400 — 1815 Lynn St.
  Arlington, VA 22209

- Write letters to public policy makers urging them to pass legislation preserving forests and wetlands, and to force reclamation of strip mined and eroded lands. Ask your classmates to do the same. You can find your representatives' addresses in the library or telephone book.

A FINAL WORD

After many years, a beautiful, useful forest is made. Unfortunately, it takes only a few years for man to destroy nature's work. The more we learn about deforestation and erosion, the more we realize that these practices must stop. They must stop because rainforests and wetlands provide needed services to humans. If you follow the suggestions in this book, you can help reduce the strain that human's have put on forests, wetlands, and other natural areas.

GLOSSARY

ATMOSPHERE: The air that surrounds the earth.

BARREN: Not able to produce anything.

BREEDING: Producing offspring.

CARBON DIOXIDE: A colorless and odorless gas that is made up of carbon and oxygen.

CONTAMINATE: To make dirty; to pollute.

DEFORESTATION: Cutting down trees for fuel or timber; clearing land for farming and settlement.

DROUGHT: A long period of time when there is very little rain or no rain at all.

ENDANGERED: In danger of becoming extinct.

ENVIRONMENT: The surroundings in which a person, plant or animal lives.

ERODE: To wear or wash away slowly.

GREENHOUSE EFFECT: The build up of gases (mainly carbon dioxide) in the atmosphere that trap the sun's heat and affect the earth's climate.

HABITAT: The place where an animal or plant naturally lives and grows.

MARINE: Having to do with or living in the sea.

ORGANIC: Having to do with or coming from living things.

POLLUTION: Harming the environment by putting man-made wastes in the air, water and ground.

PURIFY: To make pure or clean.

RECYCLE: Reusing materials instead of wasting them.

SEDIMENT: Small pieces of matter that settle at the bottom of a liquid.

SPECIES: A group of animals or plants that has certain characteristics in common.

STRIP MINING: Mining or taking minerals from the earth.

TOPSOIL: The top part of the soil that has most of the foods that plants need to grow.

TROPICAL RAINFOREST: A tropical woodland that receives 100 inches or more of rain a year.

VEGETATION: Plant life or total plant cover.

WETLANDS: Land or areas that contain much soil moisture.

INDEX

CARBON DIOXIDE   11

DEFORESTATION   7-14, 21, 29

DROUGHT   5

ENDANGERED SPECIES   26

EROSION   13, 18-21, 26, 29

GREENHOUSE EFFECT   11

INDONESIA   13

POLLUTION   14

RAINFOREST   6, 7-14, 20, 26, 29

REDWOOD TREE   14

SARIQUA DESERT, PANAMA   13

STRIP MINING   6, 21, 26

TOPSOIL   18, 19

WETLANDS   6, 15-17, 26, 29

COMMUNITY BAPTIST CHURCH
LIBRARY